NO LONGER PROPERTY OF
SEATTLE PUBLIC LIBRARY

SEP 1 2 REC'D
SEP 2 1 REC'D

D1164771

Too Sticky!

Sensory Issues with Autism

Jen Malia

illustrated by
Joanne Lew-Vriethoff

Albert Whitman & Company ✳ Chicago, Illinois

For my husband, Dave,
and my kids, Noelle, Holly, and Nick—JM

For Max, Mattiece, and all the kids with superpowers,
may you all rock the world and continue to amaze us—JLV

Library of Congress Cataloging-in-Publication data is on file with the publisher.

Text copyright © 2020 by Jen Malia
Illustrations copyright © 2020 by Joanne Lew-Vriethoff
First published in the United States of America in 2020 by Albert Whitman & Company
ISBN 978-0-8075-8026-4 (hardcover)
ISBN 978-0-8075-8028-8 (ebook)
All rights reserved. No part of this book may be reproduced or transmitted in any
form or by any means, electronic or mechanical, including photocopying,
recording, or by any information storage and retrieval system,
without permission in writing from the publisher.

Printed in China
10 9 8 7 6 5 4 3 2 1   HH 24 23 22 21 20 19

Design by Aphelandra Messer

For more information about Albert Whitman & Company,
visit our website at www.albertwhitman.com.

Holly sat on her chair and poked pieces of pancake in syrup with her fork. She loved maple syrup with her pancakes—but not how sticky it was.

If she was careful, she wouldn't get sticky syrup on her hands. But then she missed a piece. Her hand touched syrup! Holly squirmed and shook her hand in the air.

"What do you want, Holly?" asked her sister Noelle.

Holly groaned.

"Use your words," said Mom.

"Dishcloth!" Holly said.

"How do you ask nicely?" asked Mom.

"Please," said Holly with a frown.

Mom gave her a wet dishcloth. Holly wiped her hand.

The sticky syrup made Holly remember her science class would be making slime today. She worried slime would be sticky too. Maybe she wouldn't have to go to school if she ate slowly.

Holly continued eating. But then Noelle's fork slipped out of her hand and crashed to the floor.

Holly covered her ears with her hands. Loud noises hurt!

"I'm sorry, Holly," said Noelle.

"It's okay," replied Holly, like Dad taught her.

"Time for school," said Mom,
holding out Holly's backpack.
   "I don't want to go to school,"
said Holly.

"Why not?" asked Dad.

"Green slime might be sticky,"
Holly answered.

"But you love science class!" said Noelle.
"Slime day was my favorite!"

"I like experiments. But slime is made with glue, and glue is sticky. I don't like sticky things," said Holly.

"Let's ask Miss Joy if she'll let you wash the slime off your hands," said Mom.

"All right," said Holly. She reached for her backpack. Slime might be okay if she could clean her hands.

Mom drove Holly and Noelle to school. The pine trees
Holly saw out the car window looked covered in slime.

She closed her eyes and took deep breaths to relax, like Mom taught her.

When she opened her eyes, the slime was gone.

Holly walked with Mom to Miss Joy's second-grade classroom.
Mom waited for Holly to speak. But Holly stayed silent.

"For science today, could Holly have water and soap at her desk
to wash off slime?" Mom asked. "She doesn't like sticky hands."

"Of course," said Miss Joy.

Holly let out a breath.

"What do you say, Holly?" said Mom.

"Thank you," Holly said with a smile. She let go of Mom and went to her desk.

"Hi, Holly," said Nick.

But Holly didn't hear him. She heard the noise of her classmates coming into the room better than voices.

"Hi, Holly," he said louder.

Holly turned toward Nick, but she didn't
look at his eyes. They made her uncomfortable.
Holly answered, "Hi," like Mom taught her.

Throughout the day, Holly thought she saw slime everywhere.

She peeked at her green stress ball under her desk to make sure she wasn't squeezing slime.

At lunch, the green jell-o looked like slime.

At recess, the monkey bars looked like they were coated with slime too.

That afternoon in science class, Holly stared at the glue, water, and green food coloring on her desk. Miss Joy set down a cup of borax mixed with water on each desk too.

Holly loved experiments. But not today.

She didn't want to touch anything sticky like slime.

Holly added green food coloring to the borax mixture and stirred them together with a popsicle stick. She carefully mixed glue and water in a different cup with another popsicle stick.

Holly turned her head away so she didn't smell the glue. She let out a breath when she didn't get the sticky glue on her hands.

"Glue thickens the liquid to make slime," said Holly.
She liked when she could see how experiments worked.

"What does that mean?" asked Isabella.

"The thicker the liquid is, the less runny it is," replied Holly.

"Add the borax solution to the glue mixture and stir
together," Miss Joy told the class.

"My slime is thick enough to stay on the popsicle stick now!" said Holly. She was so excited, she didn't notice the smell of glue anymore. But she wanted the sticky slime to stay on the popsicle stick.

Nick and Isabella grabbed their slime with their hands. Holly stared at hers. Watching the slime thicken was fun. But since it stuck to the popsicle stick, Holly worried the slime would stick to her hands too.

"Why aren't you playing with yours?" asked Nick, holding out his slime.

Holly groaned, and Nick moved the slime away from her.

"What's wrong, Holly?" asked Isabella.

"I don't want to touch slime," she answered.

"Why not?" asked Nick.

"I don't like sticky things," said Holly.

"Shouldn't a scientist test her experiment?" asked Miss Joy. She set a bowl of water, hand soap, and a roll of paper towels on Holly's desk. "You can wash your hands when you're done."

Holly watched Nick roll his slime
into a ball. It didn't stick to his hands.

She looked at the bowl of water
on her desk. "Okay, I'll try it."

Holly squeezed her stress ball and took a deep breath. She gently poked the slime and pulled her finger away.

She tipped the cup, letting the slime ooze out onto her desk.

She picked up the slime and squeezed it softly in her hand.

"Wonderful, Holly!" said
Miss Joy. "How does it feel?"
    "Slime tickles," said
Holly, giggling.

It didn't make her fingers stick together like syrup did! The borax kept the slime from getting too sticky. But Holly still washed her hands when she was done.

When school was over,
Dad and Noelle met Holly
at her classroom door.
   "Did you make slime?"
asked Dad.
   Holly nodded.
   "That's great!"

"Did you get sticky, icky hands?" asked Noelle.

"No," said Holly. "Slime is like a solid when you squeeze it but like a liquid if you let it ooze through your fingers."

"Wow! You know a lot about slime," said Noelle.

Holly took out her container of slime. "Do you want to play with it? I know it's your favorite."

"Yes!" said Noelle.

"We'll stop at the bathroom to wash hands on the way out," said Dad.

Noelle grabbed a handful of slime. Holly took the rest. And they both giggled.

Author's Note

I know firsthand what it's like to experience the world through Holly's eyes. Both my daughter and I live with autism and sensory issues. Through this story, I hope to raise autism awareness and acceptance, especially for girls on the autism spectrum. Boys are diagnosed with Autism Spectrum Disorder (ASD) four times more often than girls, according to the Centers for Disease Control and Prevention (CDC), but that doesn't mean autism affects more boys than girls. Research by the Interactive Autism Network suggests girls with milder forms of autism are often overlooked for a diagnosis or misdiagnosed because they don't *look* autistic to the casual observer. This is due in part to autistic girls masking, or hiding, their autism, trying to blend in. They often carefully observe and later imitate neurotypical girls, repeating the language they hear and copying the gestures they see when they encounter similar social situations. For example, autistic girls might look toward faces to make it seem like they're making eye contact. They might also change behaviors that parents or friends say are unusual or strange, such as assuming certain postures, speaking in certain tones of voice, and using certain facial expressions. I know I did these things as a child and still do even as an adult. This is the main reason I wasn't diagnosed with ASD until adulthood, and why I needed to advocate for a diagnosis for my daughter. We were diagnosed with ASD on the same day; she was two, and I was thirty-nine.

Many children who are autistic also have sensory issues, like Holly. A fear of sticky hands is only one of the many challenges sensory processing issues pose; others can include difficulty handling noises, smells, or textures. One out of every fifty-nine children in the United States are diagnosed with ASD, according to the CDC. In *Too Sticky!*, Holly goes about her everyday life like other seven-year-olds. She eats breakfast with her family. She talks to her classmates. She loves science experiments. But she experiences the world differently. Situations that are simple for neurotypical children are more complex for Holly, as she faces sensory struggles at breakfast and communication challenges with her classmates. She has difficulty touching slime in her science class and must use different strategies to overcome this. With the support of her family, teacher, and classmates, Holly does not let her autism or sensory issues stop her from enjoying life. I hope that through reading about Holly's experiences, autistic kids will see a character who reflects their own perceptions of life and that their peers will learn to relate to them with greater understanding.

Slime Recipe

Ingredients

1 teaspoon borax
1½ cups water
½ cup white glue
green food coloring
2 popsicle sticks
ziplock bag

Directions

1. Have an adult mix 1 teaspoon borax in 1 cup water and stir with popsicle stick until borax is dissolved.

2. Add 2–3 drops green food coloring to the mixture. Stir to combine.

3. In a separate container, combine ½ cup white glue with ½ cup water. Stir with another popsicle stick to combine.

4. Add borax solution to glue mixture. Stir together. Then remove from bowl and finish mixing by hand.

5. Store in ziplock bag in the refrigerator.